The Eighth Day

Two Jews against The Third Reich

Holocaust, the World's Biggest Mysteries and the other Final Solution

Dr. rer. nat. habil. T. Bodan

1st illustrated edition, April 2021.

ISBN: 978-3-7534-1725-7

Publishing and printing: BoD – Books on
Demand, Norderstedt,
Germany

The victims of the Holocaust
The victims of ignorant
politicians
The victims of stupid people

Content

Foreword to "The Eighth Day"

Yes, my child has died. I mean, her body has died. Nevertheless, I cannot get rid of the feeling that still I have to keep my promise. Whatever and wherever my girl is now, I feel that she measures me on this. No matter the dead body. I have given that promise and so I have a responsibility. After all, I cannot know whether my child still listens to my every word and perhaps longingly waits for me to fulfil that task. She might wait for me to finish the work we started together a bit more than seven days ago, trying to explain the world. For all that I know, information cannot die or disappear in this universe and so, I think, also the set of information which once had defined my child still exists. She is there, somewhere, she has dignity and deserves attention. Thus, I will finish the job now. Interestingly, it isn't much I have to do myself here. The task was solved by a boy called Samuel and his father about 70 years ago. Both were killed by the Nazis in one of the gas chambers in Auschwitz. They died together in that chamber on Christmas Eve in 1944 and they were the greatest scientists of all time.

It was very difficult for me to collect all their astounding work, because often it wasn't more than some scribbled notes on the rim of an old newspaper. Something written with shaking hands in the middle of publications of other scientists of their time. More was scratched into the walls of the miserable places they were forced to live. The most important pieces of their work however, was photographed from the interior of that Reichsbahn wagon which transported them to the KZ, and finally, there was this unobtrusive sketch in that dismal room where they both died together: a gas chamber in Auschwitz.

One word about the translation from the German original into English:

The translation was done by a colleague and good friend of the author. Unfortunately, this colleague isn't a professional at translating from German into English. He isn't even good at writing. True, he has written quite a few publications and had successfully submitted them to scientific journals, but this probably doesn't count if it comes to literature, does it? Well, the author thinks, that it is the knowledge which does count more here rather than smooth formulations and nice high flying text passages. The author thinks his book, after all, is more a scientific work, rather than a story, even so it tells one. In short: the author was happy with the translation and as it is his opinion that it serves its purpose, namely, to describe the inner structure and workings of the world.

Preface for the first "7 Days"

"There was a time when I thought this book would be difficult to read and certainly just as difficult to understand. This is hardly unexpected, as the world is not easy to explain after all. Learning and real understanding are never easy. There are tasks in life that we must endure and that are horrendous, complex, diverse and as challenging as life itself. To live, is to learn for a lifetime – to which dying is also part of. That, too, is learning and – YES – it is part of life. But then the only 12-year-old daughter of a good friend read my book and started – freely, completely according to her understanding – to draw some pictures. Pictures that would show how she saw the things she had read. We scanned the drawings and inserted them in the places of the book where the little reader wanted them to be.

... and lo and behold, all of a sudden, I no longer saw the book as a heavy read. A young girl had shown me how to approach and understand it. Only a few associative images had sufficed and reading became an easy and beautiful experience. My mind once again lived through the formerly tough pages, only this time it floated pleasantly along like a feather in the warm breeze of a summer evening by the sea and finally found what it had sought in vain for so long... salvation.

This is the story of a child, a most amazing child who mastered all these tasks. And so, her life, despite its brevity, was not meaningless. And so, her life was important and valuable.

With every bit of knowledge I manage to pass on to others, I do something in memory of this brave little child; I also think of all the many other children who have to leave much too early because we are not able to help them. None of these little characters, however, was unimportant. This book tells you why.

Our existence would be somewhat illogical if we did not have a task to fulfill. So far, we were probably not

very good at recognizing this task as such, let alone to fulfill it. We will, this much is certain, leave this world without really having done anything – each of us.

But shouldn't we at least give our children a better start so that they can take stock of their lives differently later?"

excerpt from the book: 7 Days -
How to explain the World to my Dying Child? by T. Bodan
ISBN: 978-3-7526-3972-8

Day Eight

My dear child, this will now be the last and probably also the most difficult part of our "course" in trying to understand the world. This time we will not leave the math aside. On the contrary, this time, we are going to use it. Like the true big scientists, we are going to write down the equations and let them do their magic. We will try our best to let them evolve, one might say. Because, after all, we want to know how the world IS and not how we would like it to be, right?

Thereby, I do not want to adorn myself with borrowed plumes. The keys to understand the world were given to me many years ago. First there was this box. It was full with extremely old reprints of publications, scientific publications. Some of which looked so yellowed that it was almost impossible to read the original texts. But I didn't need to anyway. I knew most of these papers already. I had them in my collection. The interesting part about these papers was the handwriting along the margins and between the lines. This was still pretty readable. The topmost paper was one of those predecessor papers of Einstein's General Theory of Relativity. An old woman, not knowing herself how she had come by that box, had given it to me. She had found the carton in her attic. When opening the box and seeing the first paper she suspected the whole content to be of that – scientific – character. And so, she considered it a nice gift for me, as I was just about to become a physicist those days – a very lazy physicist by the way and – above all – extremely slow on the uptake.

As this whole Einstein theory was by far too complicated for me by that time, I only took the box out of sheer politeness and intended to get rid of it as soon as possible. A nice fire seemed to be just the right thing. I think that Einstein respectively his Theory of Relativity would still be far beyond my grasp, had it not been for the help of Samuel and his father. The two had left so many hints and additional elaborations on these papers that at some point it was almost easy to get the gist. This however, I was not to learn for a very long time. However, for some funny reason, something I'm absolutely unable to explain, I did not burn the box. I kept it with me wherever I moved. It learned to know almost all of my various girlfriends and I might even add that it learned to know some of them better than I knew them myself. It crisscrossed all over Germany, stood in many cellars and lofts and spend a lot of time in various car trunks. Why, in the end, this unobtrusive box did manage to survive in my possession, I cannot tell. I'm neither a believer not a fatalist and so, I think, it just was my laziness or the same kind of accident which one day brought me to open the very box a second time, but this time to look a bit more closely, to show a little bit more respect and to open my heart, or whatever was necessary, a tiny bit more.

There was this one day where an official guy from the local tax office had announced himself to check on our "working rooms". I had no idea what he wanted to "check on", but I thought that all rooms we had declared as work rooms and studies should also better look like some. I saw absolutely no problems anywhere except for our so-called server- and archive-room. Not that I suspected anything wrong there but, well, as the name says, it is a room where we keep the servers nobody looks at except there's something wrong. And there is the stuff being stored there for safe keeping which usually just means for good. Just as with all things you rarely see, you don't exactly know how they look like and so I wasn't sure what an impression this room would make to an overcritical taxman, especially one who was keen on justifying his job by "finding something". Thus, I decided to check on the room myself before the taxman and see whether it needed a bit of "structural optimization". Most of my anxiety by the way come from the fact that you and your siblings have played there, even when it was forbidden. And in fact, I found rather impressively huge and fairly intact ecosystems of dinosaurs, knights, Cowboys and Indians there. It must have been wonderful adventures which took place in that on first side so unimpressive, if not to say, dull room. And it is a pity that you can't tell us these stories anymore. When forcing all those knights, Indians and dinosaurs into a bag I suddenly saw the box. You had used it as small platform on which the Indians had built their home. I immediately recognized it and it almost made me feel guilty… somewhere back in my brain. And so, this time I did not just put it to another place, but opened it.

I didn't expect anything. After all, science meanwhile was years ahead and what on earth was there to learn when reading old papers others had smeared on? If I had known that there also were old newspaper rims scribbled full with funny equations in a style so very strange to me, I probably had chucked the whole package straight into the fire. Instead, I stared on the first sheet of paper in amazement and wasn't sure whether to trust my eyes. There in a funny, old fashioned German handwriting where the two words "dimension" and "Hilbert" with a question mark. Each of the two words on its own would have meant nothing to me, but together on this Einstein paper they did not only made sense but…

Something wasn't right here. This was an old box. Nobody had opened it for decades and still there was a hint about fractal multi-dimensional spaces directly on that Einstein paper. This couldn't be just an accident. Now my attention was caught.

As you well know, my little child, I have the technical possibilities to check on the age of things, especially when they are made from or contain organic substances. So, extremely careful in order not to put in impurities, I took some samples. As any material from outside the box was of young origin, such an impurity would have led to a younger dating, not to an overestimation of the age.

By the way: I had meanwhile completely forgotten about the taxman and so was completely perplexed when suddenly the bell rang and a young, well-dressed man stood in the door, showing me his ID. When slowly my brain locked into gear again, I made him a Latte Macchiato and rather boldly told him to "feel like home", because "I had no time" and was "working on something important", while I hurried back to that box checking its content and sorting it. I didn't even realize that the guy was following me. I remember him asking something about "permission to look over my shoulder", but I can't even remember whether or whether not I ever gave that permission respectively answered at all. In fact, he was a bit like a second and very quiet shadow... probably even quieter than my first one, because I did not become aware of him before he announced himself satisfied and thanked me "for such an excellent demonstration of my typical work". Meanwhile I was so deeply immersed in the content of that box that I probably didn't even say Goodbye, which, apparently the taxman did not mind at all. A few days later we received an official looking letter from the tax office telling us that – surprisingly – there are absolutely no complaints and everything is in best order. Your mother gave me a huge hug that day for the "good job I had done about this tax thing" and I never revealed to her that – if truth be told – I had not done anything to deserve that hug. So, one should note: A room declared as a work room for the tax office is most convincing if you can absentmindedly demonstrate how to work in it.

One day before the official letter, the results from the age determination measurement arrived:

"Older than 80 years – for both, paper and handwriting!"

I had expected anything, but definitively not such a number. It meant that the scribbling was mad at a time where nobody even thought about things like strings and fractal spaces not to talk about discussing it or making notes and evaluations about such ideas. Now I definitively was intrigued. I wanted to know more about those people who had left these unbelievable messages; about the content of the mysterious box in my attic…

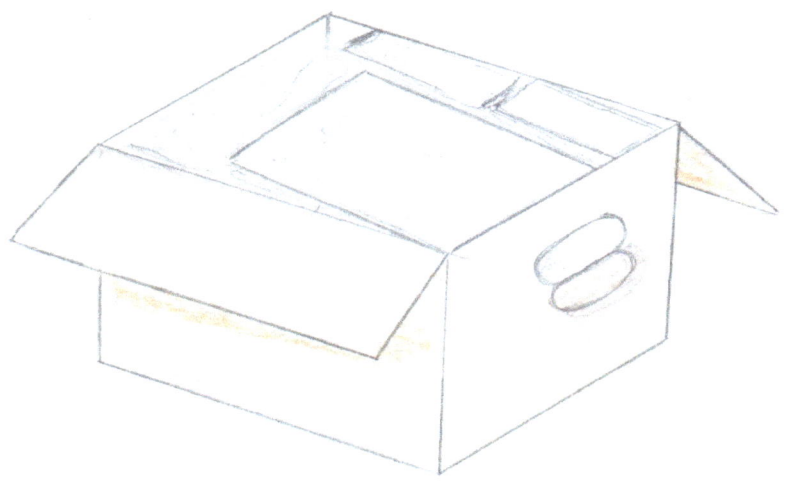

Reichskristallnacht

It happened in the night of November 9 to 10, 1938, the night hundreds of Jews were killed, tens of thousands maltreated, disseized of their property and procrastinated into concentration camps. All this happened under the watchful eyes and protection of the German police and a usually passive, often jubilating mass of ordinary German citizens. Some of whom even actively supported the pogroms. That night, Schmuel went to a meeting with old colleagues. They wanted to discuss the Einstein-Podolsky-Rosen paradox in quantum mechanics and as being an old friend of the family, he was invited to bring his son Samuel and his daughter Judith. Early in 1934, Schmuel and his son had discussed this problem with Einstein directly. As belonging to the "unwavering defenders of their home", as Einstein had called them, he even had sent them a rather personal draft with comments of the later very famous paper treating the "EPR-paradox", as it was to enter history later on. The three authors of that paper (A. Einstein, B. Podolsky und N. Rosen) had claimed that quantum mechanics can't be correct or has to be incomplete or both because it predicted a "spooky remote action effect" between well separated spatial regions faster than light. Nowadays we know that this effect is real. Many experiments have shown what we now call entanglement, but the days of Einstein, Podolsky and Rosen it only was a thought experiment and the three considered its result complete nonsense that there was a theory allowing such a thing.

While Judith, almost still a baby, played in a neighboring room with the two children of Schmuel's old colleague, Schmuel and Samuel followed the discussion of the group with severe interest. However, even though very knowledgeable in the topic themselves, they didn't actually contribute anything. This had nothing to do with them feeling anyhow superior regarding the topic, but simply with the fact that they were very conservative if it came to suggest new and rather revolutionary approaches… and in their case the approach they had in mind was nothing short of revolutionary. Some would have even declared it absolutely insane those days. Nevertheless, they felt a little bad about not telling everyone in that room what they had found out or at least suspected, especially there was a small pinch of guilt towards their host. After all, it was not without risk in Hitler's Germany, the Reich, to still stick to one's former friends and colleagues when they were Jews. But when looking at each other, both, father and son, silently agreed that the time wasn't ripe to reveal that, taking their approach, the EPR-paradox would not come as a question or a paradox, but a structural necessity of space and time.

When the riots began, their host suggested that Schmuel, Samuel and Judith simply stayed at his house until everything would be over. One might even fetch Schmuel's wife when the night was over. Schmuel felt uneasy about this, but his host didn't want to let him go and consoled him, "It is extremely un-German to attack a lonely wife and even those bastards from the SA won't dare to commit such an ignominy."

How very wrong he was he would not learn before the next day and he would carry on this failed judgment for the rest of his life.

But for the moment everyone busied her- or himself in the attempt to make the home as cozy and comfortable as possible for the three unexpected guests. The host's wife conjured a wonderful late supper and at the time everyone went to bed the atmosphere was surprisingly at ease… almost ignorantly relaxed.

In the middle of the night Samuel, who was sleeping alone on the sofa in the living room, awoke because of a timid knock on the door. After a while their host opened and a very excited voice could be heard whispering from the entrance. What Samuel now had to overhear made his inside freeze. The host and his informant quickly agreed that one must not inform their guests right now as it would probably make things worse. Then the door was closed and heavy, muffled steps sounded though the house when the host went back to bed.

Samuel's heart was racing when he silently dressed and tiptoed out of the house. He had taken the house key from a hook next to the door in order not to disturb anybody when coming back.

It was only a few hours later when he used this very key, but in these few hours he had changed completely. It was a brachial methamorphosis from a young innocent scientist into a tough and deadly warrior that had happened that night.

A courageous Jewess

They only knocked once. Sarah, even though mother of two and in her mid-forties, was still a very pretty woman and rather athletic, too. She barely had time to grab her dressing gown when the door burst open under the heavy strokes of a sledge hammer and an axe. Men in civil cloths stormed into the house.

They were from the SA, the last, the most stupid and the most disgusting kind of human beings the German community had to offer… the meanest of beasts one would find when lifting the dirtiest of stones of an already rotten society. They immediately sprang on Sarah while in the background more SA henchmen pushed in, smashing what they saw and what would not fit into those bags they had brought for valuables. When the fourth of these monsters threw himself on Sarah she got hold of one of those wooden pieces of furniture the SA-dunderheads had smashed before. With all the force she could master she hammered it into the head of her rapist, who collapsed straight away.

"Hey, this Jewish bitch is still fighting!" exclaimed one of those other SA-men. And then they came and like crazy they beat her with all they had. But in all their hatred they carefully avoided to beat her on the head or into any vital organs. Instead, almost systematically they smashed her legs, arms, shoulders and pelvis. They were nothing but cruel German monsters.

Then they put a cord around the middle of her mutilated body and hung her outside on an iron latch of the gate. Thereby they jeered and chanted their dim Nazi-songs.

"Anyone who tries to help this rag bag will be treated the same way as her, understood?" they bawled. And indeed, nobody even tried to step in. Not even the policemen who stood nearby and like so many "ordinary German citizens" only greedily stared at the naked mutilated body. Horrible moaning and heavy rasping breathing coming from the poor woman moved nobody here.

Suddenly, a loud shot rang through the night. Sarah's head was pushed to one side. She was dead in an instant. The sound of this shot was still ringing between the houses, when there was the next and the next and the next. SA-man after SA-man was hit and they fell like rotten apples from the tree. It was so fast, so precise that even after five perfect hits there was almost no reaction among the bystanders, the police or the other SA-men who had come to watch the hanging woman. This was a professional doing his job. Finally, there fell the two policemen and three of those disgusting gapers before the panic started and all hell broke loose. Simultaneously with this public tumult the shooting ended and everything was nothing more than panic running, screaming and stumbling away.

Later the German police would find the alleged murder weapon, a standard SA-carbine, near the corpse of a high-ranking SA-officer. Just as all the others of his fellows that night, he too was in civil cloths. His head was smashed, but the most peculiar thing about the situation was that usually SA-officers did not carry carbines. They had pistols and sabers. The whole case was so mysterious that in the end the Gestapo took over and covered everything up. The dead "SA-Volksgenossen" were declared victims of a freak accident and also the dead woman was registered as a victim. In fact, it was the only Jewish victim properly being recorded by booth police and Gestapo, while the latter even named her as a "potentially internal NSDAP-victim" of some high-up order.

The two brothers and the Einstein-Hilbert action

It was extremely difficult for Schmuel to get over the death of his beloved wife. And as there was no other distraction, he threw himself into the only task left: The explanation of the world. Samuel fully understood his father's sorrow. He also understood and accepted the way his father went in order to overcome the grief. He himself would have liked to spend a bit more of his time with this task, but now it was on him to care for the family, to try and protect them, to feed them in these difficult times. This was an almost impossible task. Even though it was only him, his beloved sister Judith, who he always called his "Julchen", and his father, there was barely enough food for one of them alone. The Nazi-Regime had decided that Jews must not get more than 200 calories per day which was nothing else but a cruel sentence to slow and steady starvation. For comparison: Even a sick person who is put on a strict diet would still get about 1,000 calories.

But somehow Samuel managed to keep his small family alive. With an amazing resourcefulness and irrepressible will he was able to perform the impossible… every day anew. At least he was able to provide for his sister so that she had enough almost every day. He and his father, on the other hand, had to tighten their belts and despite all the risks and the efforts it was very difficult for

Samuel to get all of them enough to eat. During his forays Samuel saw almost unbelievable cruelty and horror and it was several times when he thought he could no longer stand it, that he would rather die than to endure more of this horrible world they had to live in.

There was this one day, for instance, when he came back from his black market business outside the Ghetto, when a small boy asked him for a piece of bread. The little boy sat right next to this pile of rumble behind which the hole to the outside world was hidden. Obviously, the kid knew that here the "jumpers" came back in. There were others like Samuel who did little trading business in order to smuggle bits of food into the Ghetto to avoid starvation under this horrible dictatorship of the SS.

Next to the boy sat another one, apparently his brother. He was even smaller, even thinner than the first one, almost a skeleton. They both squatted in a pile of tatters and both seemed too exhausted, too lethargic to move. The moment the bigger of the two became aware of Samuels presence, a small thin hand came out of the pile of rags. It looked as if it was done with the last strength he could master. The thin skeletal hand moved towards Samuel and he simply stood there, shocked. The boy didn't even move his head. It was as if he already knew that they wouldn't get anything. It seemed like hopelessness and despair would have been born into this world as children and now they crouched here on this wall just about to die. Samuel just stood there and stared.

He simply couldn't move, couldn't tare himself away…
or at least his body.

Suddenly however, the smaller of the two children,
even though weaker in appearance, nothing but skin and
bone and huge, huge eyes, looked at him. He looked at
Samuel with eyes, which stared into this world from a
place far, far away and they looked at it as something of
unbelievable beauty and nameless cruelty going hand in
hand. Something this little boy never had the chance to
grasp, to explore. It even seemed like this boy internally
already knew he would never ever get this chance, but
still he was not ready to accept this.

For a very brief moment Samuel felt a shiver running through his body moving him. He felt the loaf of bread in his jacket and he suddenly thought of his mother. His mother would rather have died than to leave these two brothers, than to pass them without breaking her bread and hand a piece of it over to them. But then, in an instant, Samuel's innermost hardened again and he thought, "Yes, and because of that she is dead now!"

Then he forced the picture of his little sister, his little Julchen, into his head and it became almost easy to turn away from the sight of the two starving brothers in their dirty pile of rags. A scrawny hand slipped back under the tatters, but a pair of huge eyes was still not ready to accept the death sentence. While Samuel was turning away a mouth opened, a mouth with lips thin like paper and a funny, slightly familiar noise reached Samuel's ears. Samuel accelerated but the boy called again. Again, and again the boy called and Samuel was almost about to run, when he heard the commanding outcry of a SS-man, "Shut your damn ugly mouth, Jewish brat!" it rang through the street and Samuel's heart beat like crazy.

'Shut up, little boy,' he thought and knew the same moment it was no good.

Slowly Samuel walked on and behind him the little starving boy called again and again. There was something peculiar about his voice. In the beginning the noise he had made was hoarse, almost like rasping, but with every call it became clearer and brighter and now it was so pure that it reminded Samuel of a very fine, high-pitched and perfectly tuned bell.

"I said: Keep your bloody mouth shout! Didn't you get it?" bellowed the SS-man and Samuel couldn't help it, he had to turn and watch.

There were two SS-men, huge and terrifying with their boots, their leather coats and their machine guns.

"Hey man, look what an awful carcass this is!" Samuel heard the voice of the second SS-man, "disgusting, these vermin…"

"Why do you think you can shout into my ears?" the bigger one of the two had grabbed the boy and pulled him easily out of the pile of rags. After all it was not much weight the SS-man had to lift.

"IS THIS YOUR DAMN JEWISH LANGUAGE?" The voice was trembling in the most devilish threat Samuel had ever heard. He knew he had to go, NOW! But he could not take his gaze of that bizarre scene in front of him.

As if there were no morning and no danger in the world, the little boy made this peculiar noise again and again.

"Are you mocking me? Just you wait a second!" the big SS-man bellowed. Then he grabbed those skinny ankles of the boy and tossed him through the air like a wooden stick. With dull thud the boy's skull hit the wall and burst.

"Eww, what a mess!" said the other SS-man rather quietly, "Bloody hell, throw this away, man!"

The addressee was grinning. He threw the headless corps into the lap of the other boy, the brother, and jeered, "Well, Jew boy, look at that! Now you have something to eat!" and laughing, the two went away.

Samuel didn't hear any crying or sobbing, nothing. There was nothing than endless resignation and silence. Very slowly he turned and went home.

"I have to be stronger than my mother was!" he said to himself over and over again, while he was walking.

It was not before he was at home when he allowed himself to think about the noise this little boy had made. Without a word Samuel had put the loaf of bread on the table and then he had seated himself near the stove. Now the words hidden in this bell-like noise of the little boy were clearly in his head and his heart tightened when he finally realized their meaning. It was simply:

"Hevenu shalom aleichem!"

The boy had only wished him peace. He had wished him, Samuel Stamler, who did not want to share his food with the two starving boys, peace. This little boy had done nothing but shouted the Jewish rite of peace… and had been killed for it.

Samuel's father immediately saw that something was wrong. He looked up from a stack of crumpled papers, put the stub of pencil aside, stood up and went to his son without a word. He took him in his still powerful arms and hugged him.

Now, it broke out of Samuel. Sobbing he reported what he had seen and his father cradled him like a small child.

32

The little sister came into the room, but the father only nodded to her and so she went back to the bedroom. After all, they had plenty of space now since they became less and less in the Ghetto.

When Samuel had calmed down a bit, his father stroked his head and said:

"Come son, let us see if we still can help!" With this he stood up, pulled on his old coat, with the Yellow Star plainly visible on his chest, and went to the door. Samuel did not understand this, but he followed all the same. They went down the stairs and out into the street.

It already was curfew and if they had been seen, they would have been shot straightaway, but Samuel's father suddenly radiated such power, such reliance that Samuel simply couldn't help but calm down completely.

When they reached the spot, the headless corpse of the little boy was still lying over the lap of his bigger brother. Carful, almost like they did not want to make contact at all, Schmuel's strong hands touched the bigger boy's shoulders and shook him almost imperceptibly. Suddenly, the boy's torso collapsed and fell forward covering the corpse of his little brother. They both were dead now. Samuel began to sob again. No matter how much he had hardened himself after he had to shoot his own mother in order to safe her from further pain, this was too much for his still very young soul. Schmuel slowly, almost graciously, straightened the body again and leaned him backwards against the wall. The head fell onto his right shoulder and moonlight shone on the staved features of the boy. It was a picture of utmost resignation and sorrow, infinite sadness and pain. Schmuel let go of the little body, stood up and laid his arms around his son. He felt him shivering and said softly, "We will give them a proper burial and bemoan them like they were our own sons and brothers."

With this he bent down and carefully wrapped some of the rags in which the little boys had sat around the two corpses. Then he lifted the bigger package on his strong shoulder. Without hesitation Samuel took the smaller one and very fondly, almost like a holy object, carried it over his arms in front of him. It was extremely light. They walked slowly, like being in a procession.

"Halt!" it bellowed suddenly in front of them.

In the moonlight one could just make out the silhouette of an SS-uniform.

"It is curfew, you damn Jews!" a second voice yelled. Samuel immediately recognized that voice. Even though the man was still in the shadows and rather far away, Samuel recognized it easily. He was certain he would always recognize it. Almost no matter the volume, no matter whether his senses might not be able to detect the sound, it wouldn't help his soul from still sensing this man. He was sure that they would die now. Die like the two poor boys, whose dead bodies they carried through the streets. They would be shot or battered to death by those two monsters who directly came from hell and who still spoke the same language as he and his father, the same wonderful language they called their mother tongue. He couldn't explain why, but Samuel reflected that he somehow liked the idea of dying just now. Right in that moment he thought of all those horrible pictures in his head, the unbearable screaming, begging and those many inhuman scenes he had to witness and death appeared to offer such a wonderful salvation, such an easy way out of all this misery. He wanted this burden to be lifted off his heart and to die. He only felt sorry for his little sister, his Julchen, who would also have to die without him or father. Perhaps she would even die like the two little boys had died or she would just starve in their little flat in the middle of the Ghetto... another nameless Jewish child. Also, the wonderful interesting work he and his father had begun. They would not be able to finish it and as they never would be given a chance to publish their results, their amazing insights in proper form, it would simply be lost. Ready to die, Samuel looked at his father's broad back and he wondered. He wondered how this strong man could still walk on and calmly, like it was the most ordinary thing in the world he was doing, simply lifted up one hand.

"Hauptscharführer," he shouted with the steadiest voice, full well knowing that such a rank was at least five grades above any of those two SS-men, "Please do not shoot us before we have been able to finish the order issued by your SS-administration!"

Even if the text would have given rise to suspect, as Schmuel said it, it did not sound ironic... not in the slightest.

"What order?" asked the voice of the SS-man deep in the shadows and one could hear that there was a bit of unease ringing in it. These creatures didn't know anything but cruelty and obedience and one single, no matter how weak, unusual aspect brought them out of balance and took away from them the bit of confidence they had. Thus, Schmuel helped them and cited by heart from one of those recent official announcements:

"In the interest of the health and purity of the Volksgemeinschaft all potential sources of impurity and disease have to be removed immediately, Herr Hauptscharführer. Thus, we only dispose of these corpses, because at such temperatures... well, Herr Hauptscharführer, you probably know."

Of course, nothing did these creatures know except that corpses did start to rot and stink if being left outside after the killing was done. But they have heard the words "Volksgemeinschaft", which means the people, in connection with health and purity often enough in order to meanwhile string them together.

"Now see, a Jew who actually can work," said the SS-man in the light and actually laughed. Then he added, "Well, then in the interest of the Volksgesundheit, our people's health: Go ahead!"

Thereby he bellowed the last two words into the night, saluted and clicked his heels that it sounded like a sharp shot.

Then also the other SS-man came to a snapping attention and shouted, "Jawoll, everything for the Volksgesundheit!"

He had just come out of the shadows and Samuel could see his face while they passed. It was by far the most stupid face Samuel had ever seen. He could not help it, but suddenly he had the overwhelming feeling that he should be happy about his fate. Happy about being a poor Jew in such a miserable situation rather than being punished with being such a dimwitted monster. For nothing in the whole world, he would have swapped with this creature.

Along the way to the house was a small patch of green. Once it had been a playground for the children of the neighborhood. To this place they brought the two dead bodies. Samuel quickly fetched two spades out of the cellar of their house and then they started to dig.

When they had put both children next to each other in the pit they started singing the Lamentations of Jeremiah. They sang quietly, very quietly, it was more a humming. Because they knew what would happen if the SS caught them here, singing Jewish songs or alone doing this small ceremony for the two brothers. After that they closed the grave and went home.

They found Judith on the bench next to the small oven. She was fast asleep and the father said to his son, "You did right my son, when you preserved the loaf of bread for your little sister, but we also did right in honoring these two little boys and in lamenting their death.

Therein lies great wisdom, you must know. It is the wisdom of our believe and the reason why we have been chosen above all other people. In this also lies the reason why we have been asked so much, why we have been tested so many times and so hard. But also, why we have been crowned above all others. Do never forget this, my son!"

"Yes, father!" Samuel answered solemnly and felt his confidence coming back to him.

"Let us break bread in the morning when your sister awakes. Then we will mourn the two boys again, but now I would like to show you something."

With this he pulled his son over to the small table in the middle of the room. He signaled him to sit down and took a seat himself. In the dim light of a candle, he showed him what he had found.

"I think, the good old Professor Hilbert has made one or two simplifications too many, do you see?!" he started and in a jiffy father and son were lost in a world where no SS-men and no Hitler-regime with all its might could ever follow them. No matter how big the cruel efficiency, this REICH of Samuel and his father was not and would never be theirs.

Both sat in front of a publication of a famous mathematician from the University of Göttingen, David Hilbert. In 1915 he had shown that one could extract the Einstein field equations of gravitation, known as the General Theory of Relativity, out of a simple variation principle. When applying the principle, one mathematically "shakes" a term until it orders or structures itself such that it obtains a minimum of a unit called action. It is a bit like a sphere rolling around on a topographic surface with hills and valleys, losing more and more energy while moving on the surface and trying to find its deepest position within the topographic field. The sphere might even find the most perfect place, meaning the deepest position, if only being shaken long and carefully enough.

Now, he, which is to say Hilbert, had never given the Einstein field equations himself. After all, he was a mathematician and as such, he stopped his calculation the moment it was "obvious to see" where the whole thing would head. It was a bit like professional chess players who would not actually finish a game the moment its outcome is logically fixed.

Schmuel now showed his son the part in Hilbert's derivation where he had dismissed a term as meaningless, respectively zero, because it was a surface term one could omit according to the rules set by his variation principle.

"I think," he said to his son pointing at this term, "in reality we here have the expression which brings in the matter into the General Theory of Relativity. I mean this is what Einstein and Hilbert all the same brought in artificially later on and called it the Energy-Momentum-Tensor."

"What?" slipped it out of Samuel who couldn't believe it, "You believe they have thrown away a term and later realized that something was missing... I mean something that has been originally there all along?"

Schmuel smiled.

"No," he said in a drawn voice, "it wasn't that easy. Unfortunately! Because taking the rules of their variation principle it was absolutely fine to erase this term, but, as it seems, nature, or the universe, if you prefer, does not follow such a simple rule... well, not always anyway. It kind of finds ways around it and then, surprise: the term does not disappear and is – as I suspect – the reason for what we see, detect or take as MASS and all other kinds of matter in the universe."

"Thus, you have invented a new kind of math with a new variation principle, right?" Samuel asked in a doubtful tone.

"No," said Schmuel again, "I have not invented it! It is just the universe acting this way. The universe is simply using more degrees of freedom than Einstein and Hilbert have thought... well and this just makes the variation more comprehensive, more holistic, more CATHOLIC." And he briefly laughed about the last word.

"But how? What is the additional degree of freedom, I mean the one Hilbert did not use?"

"It is the dimension of time and space itself."

Samuel needed a while to comprehend his father's answer, to digest it. Then he asked in a tone which simultaneously revealed disbelieve and beginning understanding, "So, the universe variates more than Einstein and Hilbert assumed? Thus, it finds another, more global minimum and in the end reaches a different state than we have thought, right?"

"Yes, my son, one could put it that way," Schmuel answered. "But with the later on introduction of the Energy-Momentum-Tensor both had made up for this little "blunder" well enough, but this way matter comes in artificially while with the correct variation it would already be there."

"And when the surface term is not been thrown away and the variation is been performed differently, then the matter does come in automatically?"

"I'm convinced of it, my son, but we still have to do some work on this aspect," Schmuel answered. Then he showed his son what he had derived so far and with verve they started to work, forgetting hunger, exhaustion and misery. The goal was set. They had to find those missing pieces in the universal puzzle and then they had to put it all together.

Judith, the Little Sister

Father and son were still sitting over those papers, excitedly discussing the new world that was unfolding before their eyes, when suddenly a small hand was placed on Schmuel's arm and a timid little voice asked, "Papa, I'm a bit hungry... only a little bit. Is there something today?"

Completely surprised Schmuel and Samuel turned their heads, eyed the small girl right next to them and asked themselves how long Judith might already has been standing there. Both father and son looked with such a fondness at the girl, it was like the sun would rise again this day. Despite all the privation and suffering she still was a very beautiful little lady. She had the bright hair of her mother and together with her blue eyes she might have made the perfect Aryan, if there only weren't those Nürnberg racial laws, which made her a Jewess.

"... it is really only a little hunger...," repeated Julchen her question almost ruefully.

Immediately there came life into the two men. The father shoved the loaf of bread in front of the eyes of the little girl and simply answered, "Here my beautiful lady!"

Judith's eyes widened in happiness. But then her gaze came to rest on her brother's hand which just had slipped into the pocket of his jacket and when seeing what he had brought for them she almost yelled and clapped her hands.

"Oh, good Lord!" the father exclaimed, "Ham and cheese, how on earth did you do that again my son?"

"Well," the boy answered in a mock voice, "the ordinary Jew, after all and as it is well known, is sly and pretty good in doing business."

Father and daughter laughed, but then they were completely stunned when Samuel conjured a small glass of honey out of the other pocket of his jacket.

When they had put all the delectability on the table and Schmuel had prepared a tee out of nettle leaves he became silent and contemplative. "I would like us," he began, "to savor our food in properly kosher manner, even though the ham most likely is anything but kosher…"

With this he twinkled to Samuel, who smiled and made a skeptical face. As if to say: 'Who knows?!'

"Let us think of all the other Jews while we eat! Let us think of those who do not have such a luxurious meal as we have. Above all, let us think of those children the Nazis have driven into horrible starvation right in front of our eyes and of those we could not help, …

… no matter how much we might have wanted to."

These last words he spoke loud and clear. His daughter looked surprised, almost a bit shocked, but Samuel understood that the words were for him and sensed how much better it made him feel. Then his father spoke the thanksgiving prayer and he blessed his children and the meal… a meal he explicitly mentioned in his somewhat unorthodox prayer Samuel "had so cleverly gained" for the family.

Brief Hours of Scholarship

No matter how unbelievable it sounds, but Samuel managed for a surprisingly long time to keep the family alive. During the war his trading business got ever better. As astonishing as it seems, especially as shortness outside the Ghetto grew, the business opportunities for clever guys like Samuel became better because the black market became more and more important also for the ordinary German people. The hole in the wall, next to which the two Jewish boys had died before, thereby was his entry and exit between the two worlds.

He sometimes even made a bit of profit which would have allowed him to flee the country. Some of his partners had offered him that opportunity. Getting out of Germany, to safety, but never he would have had the heart to leave his father and his sister. And so, he stayed, did his business and took good care about his little family. It had already happened several times that his partners had warned him when there was another raid or "evacuation". This had always allowed him to hide until the storm was over and then proceed with the daily struggle for life. Usually, it wasn't a big deal for him to get new papers telling any ordinary SS-man that they were still allowed to be here, but this also was the limit of helpfulness he could expect from his partners. After all they were ordinary Germans and he was "only" a Jew. But when it came to such limits, he still was pure businessman, never asking more than "reasonable".

Soon and thanks to the war and those shortages it brought, his little business was so successful, that he found time again to help his father with the other important and much more interesting, much more satisfying task: the solution of the world's principle riddles. Especially when it came to complex and tedious mathematical derivations his father usually trusted him to cope with it. And truly he almost never made a mistake, no matter how long and cumbersome those evaluations were. He simply had a neck for these things and his unbelievable brain allowed him to overlook stretches of equations others would have needed to write over many, many sheets of papers, while he didn't even need to write them down but just noted the final results for his father.

His father meanwhile often sat in a corner with Julchen and taught her something. She too was an extremely bright child. When Samuel was stuck in a calculation, he always loved it to watch the two "doing school" and he marveled those astute blue eyes of his little sister, which hang on his father's lips. She listened carefully to every word those lips spoke and took them in in her most individual manner. Very often when watching them Samuel had an idea how to proceed with his own derivations, because suddenly a new way had come to him, one he had not seen before. All this made him sometimes see his sister as an angel, a small, skinny, sometime noisy but always lovely angel. He would have given everything for her, but he already knew he would not be able to safe her. His only wish was that she should not die like her mother died or the two boys, that it would be quick and painless… more or less. He knew he would not be able to safe a single one of them, except for himself, but to him, this was completely out of the question. He had decided it months ago that he would never leave them here alone.

One day he had bought a whole bag of books for extremely little money and had actually intended to sell them for a profit, but when he saw that they were adventure and animal books, he had given them to his little sister because he knew how excited she would be about them. She was particularly taken with Alfred Brehm's Africa stories, and once she was immersed in one of his stories about the continent that was so strange and yet so wonderful to her, she forgot the dreary world around her and a rapturous smile was on her beautiful face. Now, however, it was time for lessons and the Brehm-books lay in the corner, while the little reader sat with her father and hung on his lips as if spellbound.

And thus, Samuel once again listened to his father while he explained his little sister why things when being extremely small behaved so much differently compared to our scales. It was the basics of quantum mechanics his father was just laying out in that small room and there was an almost palpable attention radiating from the little angel to whom his father spoke.

"… now my pretty lady, there simply is no reason why there shouldn't be cosmic structures, universes also on completely different scales, you know. Your clever brother has just proved that a Friedmann-cosmos could easily be constructed in only two spatial dimensions. This cosmos, as it is tradition within the fast community of Friedmann-cosmos, would also have constant curvature when being assumed as a spherical surface."

"Don't forget: it could also be a hyperboloid or a plane!" Samuel added without being asked.

But father only smiled and drew those various geometries with spirited movements of his huge hands into the air.

"Your brother is right, of course," he admitted, "but I prefer the sphere, because with this I can easily construct the whole of our universe, which is to say, the universe we do observe."

"How can you do this, Papa?" asked Judith equally a little surprised and highly excited.

"Well, simply imagine the space full of such little Friedmann-cosmos. They are so small that we usually don't recognize them…"

"How small is that, Papa?"

"It is about ten to the power of minus 35 meters, which is the Planck length."

"Oh," Judith said, "this Planck I have heard about. Isn't this the one who actually invented quantum mechanics?"

Samuel laughed from his watching position and mockingly confirmed, "Oh yes, Planck had invented quantum mechanics and since he has had this wonderful idea, those stupid atoms with the electrons in their shells do know that they are allowed to exist. Before, they simply didn't know that, you must understand. And most important of all, since then we are allowed to exist, too."

"Oh, come on Samuel," his sister protested, "you perfectly well know what I have meant with 'invented'." But then she also had to laugh.

"And who actually was this Friedmann, by the way?" she finally asked not without hoping to gloss over her little mishap.

"This was a Russian scientist. He was one of the first, if not to say THE first, who actually applied the Einstein field equations onto the world. Thereby he also allowed the world to behave dynamic, which was quite revolutionary at his time."

"What do you mean with dynamic, Papa?"

"Oh, this just means that the world does change, it moves and evolves and so on. Einstein wasn't very fond of that idea. He had preferred a more static world… well, at least until Hubble had discovered the expansion of our universe, this was."

"And you two," Judith pointed at her brother and nudged her father, "… you two think that the Friedmann-cosmos could also be extremely small and that there are so many of it that they make the crumbs of our universe, right?"

"In a sense, one could put it that way, yes," her father admitted. "Well, and to be honest I prefer it that way, because, and that is the important point here, these little Friedmann-cosmos automatically bring in properties into the universe we actually do observe and to which there are no proper explanations otherwise."

"What properties are these?" Judith asked in a slightly perky manner.

"The whole quantum mechanics, you little silly…" Samuel added chuckling.

"Now you wait!" Judith said threateningly, jumped to her feet and threw a small, very skinny fist against his ribs.

"And…" she threatened to strike again, "how is this supposed to explain quantum mechanics?"

Samuel pretended to be hurt very badly after his sister's heavy blow and tilted sidewards off his chair. But during the fall he grabbed his sister and pulled her with him to the floor. Down there he started to tickle her, "What a stupid question this was, little sister," he said, "... although it is so simple: The thing is that all those little Friedmen **AND Friedwomen (who knows)** are extremely ticklish. Thus, they are fidgeting all the time and because of the permanent and very nasty fidgeting – **Will you stop to dither now, little sister!** – there are simply no fixed coordinates. Permanently everything is on the move and changes its properties. It is like one has to move through a room full of little dithering sisters. It is absolutely impossible to walk or even crawl a straight line in such an awful room. It's like being drunk all the time. You can't help it, you totter seesaw-like through space and time."

Giggling the little girl still saw a fly in the ointment. She intended to spill it out but Samuel had chosen that moment to tickle her again. So, the only noise coming out was cheering and more giggling. But finally, Samuel only held her fast to the ground and allowed her to speak, "But then the whole world would permanently be drunk. However, this can't be true, because one does not see the planets and stars totter trough space, right? These objects move pretty normal, er... sober?"

"Oh, my wonderful daughter, what an amazing input!" her father said. "Now you only have to imagine that the fat old Schmuel is moving through the very room with dithering Judiths. He is so fat and heavy that those little

Judiths do not bother him. He doesn't even feel them and their fidgeting and so he, I mean this clumsy oaf, lumbers though the room as if it were empty."

Meanwhile Samuel had let go of his sister and both picked each other of the floor.

"And this is it?" Judith asked a little bit disappointed. "This is the way you bring the Einstein theory and quantum mechanics together?"

Schmuel and his father contemplated each other. Finally, the father said, "Well, one small problem we still have. We still do not know how to describe the Friedmann-cosmos in such a way that it reveals its fidgetive properties in the right manner."

"Ok, if your Friedmen and Friedwomen do not want to dither," Judith suggested still a bit giggling, "then you simply have to give them a bit of space, degree of freedom as you always say, and then you have to tickle them a little bit!"

As if being petrified father and son looked down to the little girl. Both stood there, stunned and open-mouthed and almost simultaneously they both smote their right hand on their forehead.

The Evacuation

Then one morning, their time was up. From all directions military trucks moved into the Ghetto and they were trapped. SS-men jumped from the trucks and stormed the houses. Yelling, lashing and shouting they beat out the occupants. This time Samuel had not received a warning and so he had just time to hide Judith inside the small hole behind the stove and got it covered before the door flew open.

"Get out, you filthy Jewish vermin!" one man yelled and "Hands behind the head!" bawled another.

Samuel immediately obeyed. With his hands above his head Schmuel also got up from his chair, but this was not quick enough for the SS-bastards. So, one of them rammed the butt of his carbine into Schmuel's underbelly. He sank to the floor. The man who had struck him now pulled back his riffle and was just aiming when a small, almost mingy SS-man appeared in the doorway and shouted, "Stop it! "

He had a horsewhip in his right hand and even though his statue was anything but dangerous, this man was radiating pure threat.

"Not those who can still work, you idiot!" the mingy man said rather calmly and the huge SS-man with the gun immediately snapped to attention. The other SS-man retreated. Both were about two heads bigger in size, but there was no doubt in the world, that they feared the little man with his ridiculous whip, his by far too big pistol on his belt and his leather clothing. In an almost polite tone, the man now spoke to Samuel, "Are there by any chance any more members of the Jewish race in that house, Sir?"

"Not that I know of, Herr Sturmbannführer!" Samuel answered quickly and without a trace of betrayal. But the mingy one had not looked at him at all. Instead, he had suspiciously eyed his father and watched his reactions. Now the little man's eyes were scanning the room. And it wasn't only his eyes which seemed to work. It was like a small, but extremely tough and well-trained dog catching a scent.

"Well, well, well, the Jew does know the ranks. Excellent! And well done indeed!"

He turned to his fellow SS-men and said, "You see, SS-Sturmmänner, this is the reason, why you have to watch the Jews. You turn your head only once in the wrong moment and they will have grown over your head by several inches with their enormous but all the same inhuman intellect. And if you aren't careful, dunderheads like you would just have to go back to those ugly holes we rescued you from, was it a dull backyard or a stinking pigsty."

Truly featherbrained the two only answered in unison, "Jawohl, Herr Sturmbannführer!"

But then something caught the mingy man's interest and he poked in the pile of sheets of papers being spread on the table, "Oh, what do we have here?" he said, "It looks like the Jew can even write… And look what he can write…"

Visibly surprised, he studied the papers for a while and then said, "It is very interesting that you Jews, even though just Jews, have put Hilbert above Einstein. It is almost like you ordered the Jewish madcap Einstein underneath the genius German mathematician Hilbert… very interesting, this is very interesting indeed…" his voice trailed away and became an unintelligible mumbling. But suddenly it became clear again and he demanded, "You," and he pointed to one of the SS-men, "pack all this, search carefully whether you find more and take all of it into my car! Understood?"

"Jawohl, Herr Sturmbannführer!"

Now he turned to the other SS-man, "Escort the two Jews down and treat them well!

When the SS-men had confirmed the order and demandingly nodded to Schmuel and his son to go ahead, the mingy man called after them, "Hey Jews, you know what? As surprising you might find it, but with me Einstein would still be ordered above Hilbert!"

With this Samuel and Schmuel were shoved to the staircase downwards and out of the house. As it was ordered, the SS-man did not push them, he did not beat them. He strictly obeyed the command of his superior. The moment they reached the street however, a high-pitched shout came from above their heads. "Halt, you Jews!"

Schmuel and Samuel stopped and looked up to the balcony from which the voice seemed to come.

"Didn't you forget something, gentlemen?"

The mingy SS-officer held a deadly pale Judith on her wonderful blond hair and a demon-like grin lay on his face. Slowly, almost infinitely slowly, the SS-man lifted Judith up, grabbed her by the ankles and let her swing over the banister. All the time he watched, almost studied Schmuel and his son. Nobody moved, nobody made a sound. The scene was so unreal. Not even Judith said anything or at least screamed. On the contrary, she appeared like a small heroine. Hanging there high above the pave stoned street, she perfectly well knew, that it was over for her. She also knew that it would only also cost her dear brother's and father's life if she now started to cry for help. But then she would not achieve anything but kill those she loved. Almost relaxed her eyes had found those of her father when the little man finally let go of her. Falling, she closed her eyes and made no sound. Also, Samuel and Schmuel knew that they could not help her beloved Julchen and so they kept silent and didn't move. And silently they watched her fall and hit the ground with a dull thud. They even endured to watch silently when the little body spastically twitched and out of the little mouth came an unbearable gargling noise. Then the twitching ended and Judith opened her eyes. There was an almost incomprehensible calm in her gaze, which she had kindly directed at her father and brother. Then her eyes seemed to see something in the distance that no one else was able to see. A rapturous smile played around her lips and Samuel and Schmuel knew that Judith's spirit was now in her beloved Africa…

The gargling noise and the twitching did not end before another SS-man pulled out his gun and finally released the girl.

Before the End lies a way through Fractal Dimensions

"What a shame," Schmuel sighed many hours later when he and his son were cowering next to each other penned with many others in an animal wagon, "I'd loved to let her know how much her suggestion with the 'tickled space' had brought us forward."

"Yes," Samuel answered, happy about the fact that finally his father had abandoned his crushing, pondering silence. "But in a way I'm also happy that it is over for her and that it was so quick. What brave little heroine she was, I couldn't be any prouder."

And with this, eventually, he started to cry.

His father, who was already beyond tears for a long time, pulled is son into his strong arms and said, "You have spoken the wise words of a father, my dear reasonable son. Words I should have said instead, but I didn't need to, because I have you. I'm the most blessed father in the world and I'm so proud of both of you. You and your sister you have made my life worth being lived even through all this misery. There can be no higher blessing.

But now let us honor your sister in the best way we can and that is not by mourning her or praying for her. No, we can do something much more unique: With the help of her suggestion, we can solve the world's biggest riddle before those dimwitted Nazis will kill us, too."

After his father had spoken these words, Samuel stood up, wiped the tears out of his eyes and retrieved a small piece of chalk out of his pocket. His father cleaned a reasonable patch of the floor free of the dirty straw laying there. Now they had everything they needed to get started. When the first patch of floor was filled with equations and sketches, they simply moved forward to a neighboring place. The people around them never asked, they simply backed away as good as they could. Most of them even listened interested and although they seldom understood what was said they still were happy about this unusual distraction.

"This is it!" Schmuel said loudly after a somewhat elongated passage of joint evaluation on the rear wall of the Reichsbahn wagon in which they were transported towards Auschwitz. Then he almost jeered and raised his arms in jubilation. Samuel, again with tears in his eyes, but tears of joy this time, clapped his father's broad back and said, "You are right. That is the way and Judith's hint has made all the difference."

The father turned to his son, closed his arms around him and whispered, "To our little Judith, the most wonderful girl in the world!" and then, finally, he started to weep openly himself.

After a while one of the older inmates cleared his throat and asked in an extremely respectful, rather old-fashioned tone, "Please, highly honored gentlemen, may one ask what you have found out? We perfectly well know, of course, that surely it is not appropriate even to ask highly skilled scholars, perhaps scientists like you, but perhaps… and under the circumstances?"

Everybody had started to listen and all heads had turned to the old man.

The old man who had asked in that peculiar way was wearing the clothes and the dignity of a Charam, of a Rabbi of the Sephardic Jews. And this made his almost subservient tone and expression even more special. The deep respect he obviously showed those funny two men with their curious scribbling all around the wagon told all others that there was indeed something very special going on. That the two were conveying in the language of the slaughterer made the whole situation almost mysterious.

Samuel and his father looked around. It was like they only just now, in this very moment, realized that they were in an animal wagon together with many other Jews. People who were freezing, who starved, who were closer to death than to life and above all they knew they were heading towards their extermination. Still with his son in his arms Schmuel finally answered, "Please excuse our impertinence, our boldness to use the surfaces of this somewhat inconvenient means of transportation without asking for your permission. Thank you very much for still letting us do what we have done! Thank you for your help! Now we are ready to explain to you nothing less than the inner structure of the world, or…" he tilted his head a little, "let us say with great care: we put together those bricks necessary to build up the understanding of the world's structure."

The Charam was smiling. "It looks like you are a very good Ecclesiastes, my son. So please, preach to us now! Preach of the world, its inner wisdom and please make sure that we all can take as much as possible of this to our Lord."

And so Schmuel started his most remarkable and similarly his most important lecture of his life. A lecture being considered a sermon in the eyes and ears of his audience, the last and most important sermon of their lives. As he had taught Judith, Schmuel began with the smallest. The smallest, he elaborated, we would be able to recognize but which wasn't the smallest in the world, because we'd only be able to "see" those things on our scale. He explained that in fact there are smaller things "going much deeper inside" and bigger things "going much further out". Even when using all the resources our portion, our scale of the universe has to offer, we would not be able to leave that very scale, neither to see the SMALLER nor to reach the BIGGER, but still, we do feel its influence. He stood in the middle of the wagon, sometimes holding on to one of the wooden pillars, while Samuel walked around and pointed at various sketches and drawings the two had made earlier in order to illustratively support what his father was just saying. When they moved through the topics and Samuel had to get from one drawing to another, the people in the wagon backed away again when necessary, so that everybody was able to see what Samuel was showing. Here and there he even added something while his father was explaining certain features of their findings. It was an arrow here or a line there. The people were extremely careful not to obliterate any of those figures, equations and sketches when moving.

"But," Schmuel added with a smile at his wonderful audience, "we still can learn a lot about these other regions, these other scales. Even though we cannot reach them ourselves we still get influenced by the stuff which is outside our possibilities."

"But how?" asked a deep voice.

"These boundaries…" Schmuel made a brief break and pointed in a certain direction at the wall. Immediately this area was cleared free of the people in front. "Thank you! I appreciate that!

These boundaries are not fixed. As you can see, my son has drawn them pretty scrawly and you have to believe me, this definitively was on purpose."

The people laughed.

"They are permanently on the move, these boundaries. They are fidgeting all the time and this gives us what science meanwhile has named quantum mechanics. Thus, behind this funny word isn't much more than the fact that, if looking more and more closely, space is granular. And the grains are moving all the time, which is bringing about all those peculiar things like radioactivity and which also allows certain things to exist, like stable atoms, for instance, which is to say: in the end, the granular structure seems to be necessary to allow something as funny as **us**."

"And what about those boundaries above, I mean to the bigger?" the deep male voice asked again. It belonged to a bearded giant directly next to the door.

"Is there God?" asked a child right next to him.

Schmuel smiled and with a nod of his head he sent his son in another corner of the wagon.

"Well, little boy… Ah what is you name by the way, I mean if it is allowed to ask?"

"Benjamin… Benjamin Baum, Sir," the little one replied politely.

"Ah thank you, but I meant the little boy next to you!" and Schmuel moved his gaze from the boy to the bearded giant.

Everyone in the wagon laughed and Schmuel proceeded.

"To be honest, personally I do not think that God his lurking or even hiding behind such boundaries. I rather think, he is simply everywhere and these boundaries do not exist for him because he is defined on them. Or let us put it this way:

He is all this!"

He let ring these words a short while before he went on, "Please note, this is only what I believe not what I know. But I know that also the upper boundaries do fidget. But they do it in a tardiness and strength we cannot measure or recognize directly. But we think that the fidgeting upper boundaries brought about the necessary disturbances which in the end formed galaxies, stars, planets and us. Without those perturbations namely, the universe would still be nothing but a uniform, homogeneous and boring gravy... a very boring gravy..."

Again, everybody in the wagon laughed.

"But as we all, I mean all of us in that room, and I explicitly exclude those dimwitted Nazis outside, as we all can see..." more laughter, "... luckily, we don't have such a boring universe filled with a probably rather tasteless gravy, right Benjamin? Or do you think that we all are nothing but boring gravy?"

"No, Sir!"

"Or perhaps a boring porridge... maybe with a little bit of sugar?"

"No, Sir!" the little boy said with a surprisingly strong voice and the bearded giant tenderly stroked the boy's almost bold head.

The laughter was getting louder again and Schmuel gave them time. Also, there was a little bit of whispering and separate discussion going on here and there. Finally, Schmuel raised his hands above his head and in an instant, it became quiet again. Only the rattling of the train and the whistling of the wind from outside could be heard.

"Well, now you might like to ask how we, I mean how my son and I have derived all this, right?"

They nodded, almost in unison.

"I could make it easy for me and say: Well, you can see it scribbled all around the walls and on the floor here. You don't even need to turn pages, lift stone plates or role out endless sheets of paper. The only thing you need to do is turning you head here and there."

They had gotten the wink about The Ten Commandments and the Torah and laughed again. The Charam even clapped his hands and cried out, "What a wonderful sermon this is, my son!"

He looked so happy and his eyes were so bright that Schmuel couldn't help it but think of the Holy Ghost of the Christians who must have gotten into the old religious Jew and with this thought in his mind he had to laugh himself. Then he looked the old man straight into those bright eyes and simply said, "Thank you!"

Only when the word was out did he realized how good those words of the old Rabbi felt.

"But of course, we are not going to make it so easy for us," Schmuel finally proceeded.

Without the need of his father's help, Samuel went to a stretch of floor in the middle of the wagon. Whereas his father was explaining, he pointed to a drawing he had made there earlier.

"To be honest, we needed quite a while to make those little Friedmann-cosmos do what we have liked them to do, I mean them to do what we see, to make them bring about all the quantum mechanics we detect. Then one day, I elaborated the whole thing to my wonderful 7-year-old daughter and she simply answered: '… why not giving them some space and tickle them a bit!' Yes, this is what she had suggested."

Again, the people laughed but they laughed very silently in order not to miss anything.

"We already knew that one needed to make the surfaces of the Friedmann-spheres curl in order to get to the right dither, but we had no idea how to do this in a mathematically feasible manner. Which is to say, we didn't know this until our Judith, our little heroine, showed us a way.

After her hint, it was almost easy. Instead of describing complicated geometrical surface variations for our Friedmen and Friedwomen…" laughter, "… we simply allowed those surfaces to be anything else but surfaces. Yes, in fact to be something in between a line and a surface or a surface and space… which is to say a thing with a fractal dimension."

A murmur went through the room. The people looked at him as if he had just said the craziest thing in the world and Schmuel, who had anticipated this reaction, simply stood there and smiled.

"This is much less crazy than you might think," he explained calmly. "Just have a closer look at those lines in our drawings here. From far away they are lines, which is one dimension, as you probably already know… and if you did not know it, you do know it now. But when getting closer you will see that these lines also have a certain width, right? Thus, they are surfaces and no lines. And now, when you are getting ever closer and also wear the right spectacles…" general laughter, "… then you will recognize that the apparent single surface is nothing but a collection of several surfaces. Between which you find patches free of any color. Still even closer and perhaps magnified under a microscope, you find ever smaller surface dots and so on until you will reach the scale of molecules and atoms. And as we all know, atoms are also not just spheres, right?"

"No, Sir! These are not just spheres!" little Benjamin hurried to answer and everybody laughed.

"So, instead of constructing complex and complicated curls on those surfaces of the Friedmen and Friedwomen we simply use the dimension as additional degree of freedom allowing us to consider rather generally perforated, fractured or roughed surfaces, if you like.

The interesting thing now happened the moment we had incorporated this fractality into the Einstein field equations."

Here Schmuel made a brief pause. His gaze moved over the crowd who sat there like petrified, completely still, but at second glance in full alert. "Suddenly the time appeared as nothing else but the variation of the dimension, you see?!"

Schmuel now did not see these people as an audience anymore. These had become his students and they were the best he had ever had.

"The fact the little Friedmann-cosmos, the Friedmen, Friedwoman or – who knows – Friedmaids as Judith liked to call them…" giggling, "… the fact that these things are a bit undecided about how to actually be dimensioned on the surfaces, that is to say they permanently jiggle around

70

the property SURFACE, which is to say around the two-dimensional being, does bring the appearance of time for us."

There was such a tension now, one would have heard a hair fall to the ground if it weren't for the noises from outside and the rattling of the wagon.

"And something else is happening now: The properties, the Friedmen and Friedmaids are now taking on are exactly those we observe in our quantum mechanical world."

"And above?" asked again the deep voice of the bearded giant, who meanwhile held little Benjamin in his strong arms. His face showed such a tension that it gave the impression of a source of some strange light or warmth. His voice was suddenly of a supernatural kind, as if to come from everywhere. Schmuel smiled. He was so infinitely happy about this excellent audience, these wonderful students and scholars. He knew these were his last and best.

"At the boundaries of our own universe, which is our own Friedmann-cosmos as a matter of fact, it is the same thing. There, too, we find fractal surfaces, a fractal hypersurface, to be more specific. And this will determine the quantum mechanical properties or appearance in the world or scale above, while the signals and influence from there have brought about the structures we see here. I mean the galaxies, stars, planets and us."

"Then we and the whole cosmos are only like the layer of an onion, Sir?" little Benjamin asked, disappointment in his voice.

Samuel couldn't help it. He had to laugh out loud. But then he came to assist his father and said:

"But yes, you are perfectly right little man. But why do you think this is something to be disappointed about? If truth be told there are even more layers, we think. Infinitely many to the smaller scales and infinitely many to the bigger and to make things even more complicated there are probably even more of these layered onions, infinitely many probably. And all of which are likely to be full of Friedmen and Friedmaids."

"And still, little man," Schmuel now added, "this doesn't make you one single bit less important. It does not make you insignificant. Although you are only a being on one scale in one of those many universes or parts of the universes, in one of those Friedmen and Friedmaids and although there are infinitely many scales up and down and so on, **you are special**. Because only this one being, this boy named Benjamin, has just asked this wonderful question. Only you have just created the perfect comparison with the onion. We all, my son Samuel, me, all the people in that wagon and the whole universe have to thank you for that!"

With these words Schmuel and Samuel in unison bowed to the little boy whose eyes now radiated like little stars and whose face brightened as if being just gifted with internal life.

"It is those little things which make us special and important and here and now it is you, you Benjamin Baum, being special and important."

In this moment, Samuel remembered those words his father had spoken after they had buried the two little boys on that old playground and he added, "Therein lies great wisdom you must know. It is the wisdom of our believe and the reason why we have been chosen above all other people. In this also lies the reason why we have been asked so much, why we have been tested so many times and so hard. But also, why we have been crowned above all others. Do never forget this, my brethren!"

Schmuel had now finished his lecture. He was so proud of his son to have chosen this moment to repeat those words he once had said to console him. Now his son had used the same words to comfort many people about to die and he had performed it like a grown-up man, a very wise man. Schmuel knew that there was still one piece of puzzle yet to be found, but he didn't want to spread such technical difficulties here. In this he could be rather conservative. Like an old-fashioned teacher, he took for himself the right to send his scholars away with a few questions, a few degrees of freedom or voids to be filled with individual interpretation.

This time it took a while until the audience started to move. But then the old Rabbi suddenly simply said, "Amen!"

He started to sing the "Avinu Malkeinu" and everybody in the wagon joined in immediately. Yes, they even heard them join from the other wagons and so it was like a wondrous train of salvation moving irresistibly towards death.

www.youtube.com/watch?v=0YONAP39jVE

It was the most wonderful singing Samuel and his father had ever heard and they started to weep again. And again, it was out of pure joy and gratitude.

When the train reached the ramp of Auschwitz almost all surfaces in the wagon were full with writing and sketches. And although the people were exhausted, tired and enervated they all tried as hard as possible not to step on those equations and symbols in order not to destroy them. They did not know in this moment that the wagon and the rest of that train were about to go back to the Reich in order to fetch more Jews. More Jews should be transported to Auschwitz to be annihilated there. But this transportation would never happen.

*

A short while after the train has reached its destiny in the Reich, US-forces had conquered the city and the very train station to which the train had been brought. A young officer couldn't believe his eyes when he saw the inner walls of the wagon after an excited private had called him to have a look. This young officer was a studied mathematician and a very good one, too. He was given the chance to work on a top-secret project later becoming famous as the Manhattan project, but his whole family had a military tradition. Almost every male member of that family had served in the army and so he did not want to break with that tradition and joint the "real forces". And after having come so far, he did not regret his decision. It might sound strange to some people, but this young mathematician preferred to be at the front, in the real war rather than in a safe office at X-site as they have called the Oak Ridge Laboratory in Tennessee, where they built a super bomb.

He too was stunned when seeing the drawings and the writing all over the walls and on the floor. This was far beyond his understanding. But he recognized certain parts and sensed that there seemed to be a connection between quantum mechanics and General Theory of Relativity. Thus, he called for his camera, took dozens of photographs and noted down its original positions within the wagon in a small leather-bound note book.

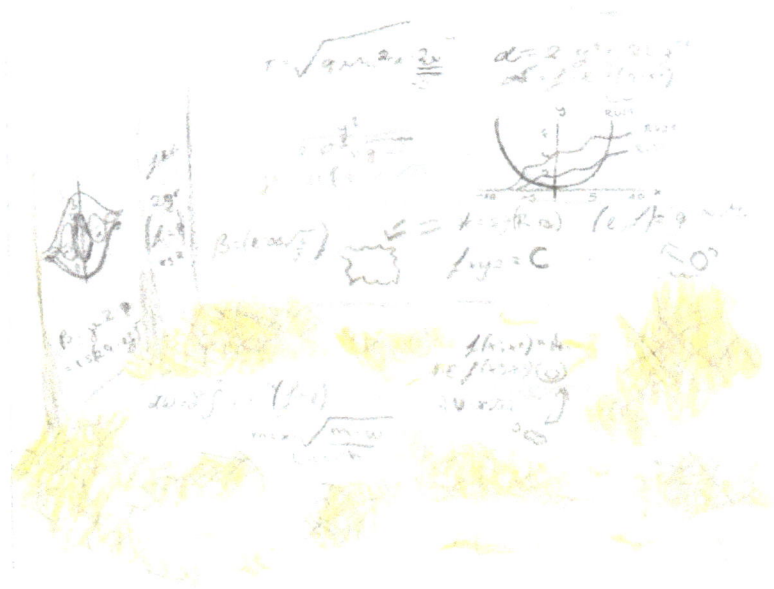

The Last Piece

Samuel and his father were deaf and blind regarding all those cruelties, the suffering and the death around them. Yes, they even almost completely ignored all those atrocities done to themselves. They were too busy to note and to care about them. Being pushed in a certain direction on the selection ramp they had discussed a certain problem and they had deepened that discussion when being forced to a wing where they were told to undress. They ignored the sanctimonious elaborations about now being cleaned from lice and disinfection in the KZ-shower. They knew that they had only very little time left and the stupid trial to cover the cruel killing by gassing somebody with Zyklon B and call it "disinfection" only insulted their paramount intellect. They simply read the signs, combined the information at hand, knew what was coming and still had much better things to worry about than their approaching death. They did not worry more about this than they needed in order to estimate the time they might have left to finish their task. If only one of those self-proclaimed "Herrenmenschen", the dimwitted watchmen, would have known what a divine stroke of genius was being performed right in front of the eyes of those blind SS-men, he had immediately shot his comrades and then asked to be gassed himself simply out of shame. But none of these monsters even had a clue. Nobody sensed anything, not even the Kapos, who were other inmates that were forced to help the SS doing the killing. Nobody wanted or could see, hear or feel anything.

And the victims?

I have no idea my child, because I was not there. But there was a lot of space just around Samuel and his father when they later opened the gas chamber. In all this inhuman crush, the suffering and dying, the people had made space for the two. And so, they had been able to leave a final message, scratched into the inner wall of the gas chamber in which the Nazis killed them.

How do I know that?

There is a peculiar entry in the "daily Vernichtungsprotokoll", the Nazis kept the minute with great bureaucratic accuracy. It reports about "two wondrous male cadavers". And there were also the other inmates. Many of them in danger of being sent to the gas themselves any day. Many of them even hoped to be salvaged from the horror this way. But that very day, some of them felt a kind of salvation which was much stronger than any death and when the KZ was finally liberated on January 27, 1945 they told their liberators about that day. They told them a peculiar story about God having shown himself to them in the most unlikely place there was in the world, the extermination wing in Auschwitz.

This scribbling in the hard concrete wall, using a broken fragment of a glazed tile, was the coronation of their work. Proud, indescribably proud they were in the view of what they had achieved. They looked at each other, father and son, knowing that they would die now and still they were happy and completely at ease. It was Christmas Eve in the year 1944 and there they stood: the greatest scientists of all times, father and son, looking at each other in a gas chamber of Auschwitz and there was nothing but happiness. They had found their equation. For them it did not matter that they were not given the chance to announce their result to the world of mankind, because they knew that information could not get lost in this universe. A time would come where somebody would recognize and combine their conclusions and complete them, making things possible which today would appear as magic. If somebody would have asked them just in that very moment whether they would have preferred a different life, they might have just answered with a plane NO. Of course, both might have wished for a little less misery and suffering for all those close to them, not such a sudden and cruel end for their little Judith, not this painful horrible death of their mother and wife, the two little boys in the street and their fellow prisoners in that wagon and here in this room. They watched little Benjamin Baum being hugged for a last time by this bearded giant, saw a very tired looking Charam… but for them, this was all just sad. Perhaps it was this sadness and all the suffering, the cruelty of a Nazi Germany and the atrocities this system did to the Jews which was the trigger for them to do what they had done, to achieve what they had achieved. So how could they be sorry for themselves?

Hitler and his dunderheads, they might have killed Millions of them; but by doing so the Nazis created the platform for two geniuses and made them able to perform what even the "Tausendjähriges Reich" (thousand year-long German kingdom) and an immortal Hitler could never ever have done and what this horrible regime also could not destroy. It was the greatest contribution to mankind's task in this world, the reason why mankind was allowed to exist in the first place. This way and pretty much unwillingly, Hitler and his Nazi-henchmen helped the Jewry to fulfil what was said in the bible, in the Old Testament, helped to truly become the chosen people... not by choice of a God, however, but by their own deeds.

In this very moment Hitler had already lost. His defeat was so complete and so deep, the outcome of the whole war would not have mattered anymore. He was nothing, a complete nobody, a necessary boundary condition, that was all. And after he and his Nazis had served their purpose there was nothing but a stain of dirt in the universal book of history. While the Jewry shone bright and clear, the Nazi regime lay dying on the floor, a set of information the universe had no use for ever again.

Almost as a byproduct Schmuel and his son had also achieved a victory over the Hitler regime no military forces could have achieved. They had destroyed its soul, its own inner reasoning. No matter when and whether mankind would see and understand this, the universe knew and this was what mattered.

The father took his son into his arms and kissed him on the forehead.

"Thank you, my son!" he whispered. "You have made me the greatest present in the world. Now I know I can go without fear. I know that I will see you again and we both know where this path is leading us."

Again. he hugged his son and sobbed. But this was out of pure happiness.

"Now I have to make you a present in return," the father whispered, "for those Christians killing us today, this is a special day where they make presents to each other. My present will come from the depth of my soul and it is the best I can give you under these circumstances."

J. Cash „hurt"

www.youtube.com/watch?v=L_gytJd6PsE

Samuel nodded. His head resting on his father's chest he didn't say a word. In the background there was the opening of a hatch in the ceiling. Children, mothers, fathers began to cry, here and there was the hushed whisper of prayer, people lost control over their bodies and some simply collapsed out of mortal fear. They all knew now what would come. From a small metal cylinder the Zyklon B crystals were dumped through the hatch into a robust steel grating. Then the hatch was closed and above all the human noise, the cries and yells one could make out that devilish fizzling coming from the crystals exhausting their deadly load into the air.

"Thank you!" Samuel whispered and he made his weak body as relaxed as possible. He willed himself to make it easy for his father and with a quick powerful twist of his arm Schmuel broke his son's neck so that he would not have to suffer. Only now the father handed himself over to his sorrow over the son he had to kill. He held the dead shell of the wonderful young man in his arms and within all his mourning he didn't feel his body passing away. He only thought of the wonderful time they have had together and he recapitulated their great work. This made him feel light and airy and full of pure joy.

*

In the protocols of that day there was a very peculiar entry by the camp doctor. It was about two male corpses, probably father and son, both with such a bright and honest smile on their faces that the liquidators did not dare to touch them. When then the Kapos came to beat them for their disobedience they also stopped and just stood there, completely shocked. Nobody had ever seen anything like that after a gasification with Zyklon B. What was more was the fact that even though the chamber was full to bursting point, the dying people, despite their own agony had managed to keep a lot of free space around that couple of father and son. When an SS-man finally came to check what was all the hold up about he almost froze when seeing them. After a while of expressionless gazing, he called for the camp doctor in panic.

In that moment a group of six detached themselves from the other awed liquidators and moved towards the two dead men. For a moment completely ignoring the SS and the Kapos, they lifted father and son with great dignity and in an almost perfect procession they marched them to the lift. Nobody moved. At the lift the six arranged the dead bodies such that father and son could face and smile at each other. Everybody took off his hat and stood still. Even the SS-man who had called for the camp doctor earlier stood in attention. It was said that he had shot himself the same evening.

About the Background of "The Theory of Everything" and "The World Formula"

by Dr. rer. nat. habil. Norbert Schwarzer

Can it be that an old box of papers from over 80 years ago, hidden for more than half a century in the attic of a godforsaken old house in east Germany contained all the necessary hints to find the "World Formula" or "Theory of Everything"?

Can it be that these papers originally belonged to two Jews, father and son, who were killed by the Nazis during the Second World War?

Two Jews, who had already been about to find the "Holy Grail of Science", long before others even thought about this problem, but then, briefly before they could finish their work, had been gasified – like so many others – in Auschwitz.

A story by far too horrifying and fascinating to be true, right?

And yet here it is, a book which brings the two things together, the story of the two Jews and the derivation of the "World Formula"…

Norbert Schwarzer:

ISBN 9789814774475
Published 2020
216 Pages

ISBN 9789814877206
To be published 2021
450 Pages

Published by Jenny Stanford Publishing

Thereby the author clearly claims that he was not the one who found the World Formula. This job was already done over 105 years ago by the German mathematician David Hilbert. But apparently, nobody had seen this. The author also explains that the nudging he had needed to start his research on the matter did not come from himself. It was the box of old papers, fallen into his hands as a pure accident, which gave him all he needed. It was the work of the two Jews, which the author prompted and pushed into the right direction. His job wasn't more than putting it all together.